FATE OF THE FATES

Also by Alexandria Blaelock

SHORT STORY COLLECTIONS
The Histories of Hayward Hall
Lovelorn, Lovestruck and Love at First Sight
Common or Garden Variety Heroes
Case Files of the Wilkinson Detective Agency
Unavoidable Fates
Christmas Travesties
Five Faces of Felicia Clarke
Little Place Called Home
Security Directorate Dossiers v. 1.
Security Directorate Dossiers v. 2.

FICTION
That Love Nonsense
Taipan vs Brown
The Ghost and Ms Cox
Friends Like That
Weaving the Wildwood
Wolf vs Orb

MS BLAELOCK'S BOOKS
Stress Free Dinner Parties
Signature Wardrobe Planning
Holistic Personal Finance
Minimally Viable Housekeeping
Planning a Life Worth Living

PICTURE BOOKS
Australia Felix

SELECTED SHORT STORIES
Alma's Grace
Blood and Bloody Profanity
Cancelled by the Cartel
Dingo Hunting
Honoris Virilis Respectu
Mince Pie Mystery
Remains of Christmas

FATE OF THE FATES

ALEXANDRIA BLAELOCK

BlueMere Books
MELBOURNE, AUSTRALIA

For permission requests, please contact
enquiries@bluemerebooks.com.

Ordering Information:
Discounts are available on quantity purchases. For details, contact orders@bluemerebooks.com.

Fate of the Fates/Alexandria Blaelock
paperback ISBN: 978-1-922744-94-4
digital ISBN: 978-1-923083-09-7

Book Layout © BookDesignTemplates.com
Cover Art © Warm_Tail licenced from Shutterstock.com

FATE OF THE FATES

Claudia put The Book of Fate aside, sighed, and pulled her red fox fur coat more closely around her. Then shook her long strawberry blonde hair around her for another layer of warmth.

Sure, it was nice enough, high up in the mountains, the air crisp and clear, and you could see for miles and miles around you.

As long as you didn't mind that the view was mainly snow, that the air was cold and crisp against your cheeks, and that the chill seeped into your bones no matter how many layers of clothes, or hair, you piled on.

Even the sound of birds flying overhead, and animals scurrying along the ground fell like stones; with a thud, disappearing into the snow's silence.

The two-room chalet she and her sisters lived in was mostly sealed against the wind, just the odd squeal as the wind gusted at speeds almost impossible to comprehend.

One of the rooms was full of Books; the sacred records of people's lives - past, present and future, this universe and all the others.

They lived in the other room.

Their beds were tucked under the eaves, closed in by doors that made the room look neater, kept the beds warmer, and provided an added layer of insulation.

Inside each cupboard, storage shelves were built into the walls at the end of the bed, and drawers for storing clothes underneath them.

The wooden walls and ceiling were dark with centuries of soot, waterproofing and use. The tiny windows set high in the walls.

In the centre of the room, was a fire.

Not like in the old days when the smoke from the open fire hung in the ceiling, but in a proper steel stove with a proper chimney that drew the smoke up and away.

Upon which a pot of venison and vegetable stew gently simmered filling the air with a delicious savoury fragrance.

Which almost completely hid the smell of dried apples, sultanas and cloves gently reconsti-tuting in another pot of water.

It was almost exactly perfect for a romantic get-away.

Aside from the never-ending presence of her sisters, and the complete absence of, well, a man.

Claudia allowed herself to dream a little about that nice blonde boy. Wherever it was he'd turned up. Somewhen in the middle of a dead-end red desert.

And then she looked at her sisters... No matter what, they couldn't compare.

Claudia was the youngest, Laura the middle, and Agatha the eldest. Though given they'd all been alive longer than time, that wasn't saying much.

Laura, her long black hair neatly pinned up and out of the way, currently dressed in black wolf skin, was polishing the measuring stick she used as a walking stick.

She'd been involved in some kind of accident before Claudia was born, and about which she refused to speak.

Agatha's short white bob brushed the polar bear coat she was wearing, making her look like a bear herself.

A fair warning to anyone else, as Agatha ate her prey alive as well.

Not literally of course, but she had a streak of ruthlessness about her, and it was best not to get on her bad side.

Though that wasn't entirely her fault, just something to be expected of someone whose job was to determine the time and circumstances of death.

As usual, she was sharpening her shears with a whetstone, the rhythmic snick, snick, snick of it loud in the quiet room.

Claudia stood up and took a step towards the stove to stir the pot of stew.

Tempted to eat just for something to do.

"Aren't you tired of sitting around here waiting for something to happen?"

"Not at all," said Agatha, "I'm happy just to be. Quietly, without any fuss."

Claudia rolled her eyes, but Agatha smiled insultingly sweetly.

"We're cosy enough here, and it really feels like we've been rushing around forever," said Laura.

"For heaven's sake! We could be doing noth-ing just as easily somewhere warm."

Her sisters started laughing.

"What?" said Claudia, but they just laughed harder.

"What?" she said, starting to get annoyed.

"Ah dear," said Agatha wiping her eyes, "we were just talking about when you'd be ready to leave."

"I won," said Laura, "hand it over," and Agatha fished a coin from her pocket and put it in Laura's outstretched hand.

"You're so predictable," she told Claudia.

"Where do you want to go this time?" Agatha asked.

"I don't know," Claudia's shrug was almost invisible under the fur, "somewhere warm. Maybe a beach?"

"Ah," said Laura, "we haven't been to a beach in a while."

Agatha grunted, though whether that was in agreement or not was another matter. "Perhaps somewhere uninhabited?"

"I'm not sure there's anywhere left that doesn't have someone living there," said Laura.

"There must be somewhere," said Agatha, "I'm not going unless there's no one there."

"I'll look into it," Claudia said, fluffing up her bedding, climbing into the cupboard and shutting the doors.

For a while, she heard them continuing the conversation as they prepared the chalet for travel, bickering amiably.

"Wouldn't you like to split up and take a vacation on your own one day?" asked Laura, banking the fire and tucking the pots underneath the stove.

"Hmmm, maybe. We'd need to go somewhere populated for that, and I'm not sure I could deal with so many people anymore." Agatha made the beds and tidied the sleeping cupboards.

"Could be fun," Laura swept the floor, sweeping the dirt and dust out into the snow.

"Maybe next time," Agatha opened the door to the book room, but as they hadn't used it for a while, it appeared in order.

And then they were done, they retired to their own beds to wait.

《《 • 》》

What Claudia hadn't told her sisters, was that the nexus was an ever-increasing network of universes.

Not just one.

And in all those universes, there was only one Claudia, but there were many many universes with and without versions of her sisters.

Perhaps because she was the only one in all the universes who wove the threads of fate into the full, glorious tapestry of life.

Or as some would have it, wrote the complete story of the universes.

That was what the book room was all about - hiding the life records where no one would think of stealing them.

Wherever they stopped they sold books for the money they needed to buy the other things they needed to survive.

Which wasn't much because the living room always reset to containing the things they needed to survive.

And they didn't sell THE books, but sometimes other books that Claudia brought from other times and places depending on what people needed at the time.

All those universes were getting a bit out of control, and she could really do with some help on that.

As each year passed, the universes expanded, and it got more and more difficult to find places they hadn't already visited. Though on occasion, if one universe deviated too much from its original root, she took the risk.

Not that it was chaotic as such in the nexus, but she enjoyed the time away from her sisters. There's nothing worse than being the youngest, forever, with older two sisters who are always picking on you, thinking you need to be monitored or instructed one way or another.

Even more galling when she had the power to erase them. Who cared about measuring or cutting when she could pull their threads out by the roots? Not that she wasn't tempted sometimes.

And they thought they were so smart...

Then again, she'd never told them she could travel the threads.

They knew she had something to do with it, but assumed the gods used her to send them where they needed to be, rather than her picking some more or less random place that looked nice.

The last few years she'd been searching for a copy of herself. Perhaps one she could swap with.

Or failing that, a nice man to live his life with while her sisters waited for her to come back.

They thought it just took the space of a nap, say an hour or two, but she'd been experimenting and had stayed away for six months without them noticing the difference.

It had been exhilarating. And liberating. And she wondered how long she could get away with this time.

She picked a thread at random and dove into it.

《《 • 》》

As always, her sensed returned slowly.

She heard booming, and for a moment was alone with the sound, trying to identify it.

The sound of surf crashing to the shore.

And then she heard seagulls squabbling.

She noticed she was warm. Too warm in the fur, but not quite awake enough to throw it off.

A sliver of blue sky through a gap in the wall.

The hint of some kind of herbal foliage blown in on the breeze through the gap.

And a little while later, the sound of her sisters talking, which was disappointing as she'd hoped to avoid them this time.

"Nice place," Laura said before taking a loud sip something, "house isn't bad either."

Agatha grunted in agreement. "How's Claudia?"

"Seems fine. No real way of telling."

"I'm worried by how much harder it seems to get each time."

Laura sipped again, "me too. I'm not sure what we can do to help her though."

"Is it something to do with The Book of Fate, or is it something she somehow figured out how to do on her own."

Laura shrugged, "no telling. But I can't help feeling like she needs some time on her own. A vacation of a sort."

Agatha grinned, "not like when we were young eh?"

"Speak for yourself, I'm not *that* old thank you very much."

"I suppose we could ask that old goat, whatever name he's going by now."

Claudia didn't care to hear anymore, and certainly didn't want them trying to fix her on what she'd hoped *would* be her vacation.

She struggled to get up, and out of the cupboard, and instantly her sisters were there to help her.

Out of the cupboard, into some fresh, clean, lightweight clothes and into her chair with a mug of tea and a bowl of venison stew.

Thankfully they didn't say anything, knowing she'd be out of sorts for a day or so after she'd moved them.

Never much for tact, Agatha said, "we're going out to see where we are."

And Laura, ever conciliatory, "you rest and we'll be back before you know it."

Claudia knew they'd be gossiping about her and plotting to visit "the old goat" whoever that was. She certainly didn't want any help from whoever he was.

But she'd have to stay for at least a week to get her strength back.

She took a sip of tea and looked around.

The structure of the room remained the same, but the walls were a bleached light wood and clean. The door and the large windows had been propped open to show a view of white sand, blue sky and turquoise ocean.

Tall trees grew down to the pristine white shore.

Setting aside the tea, she ate the stew.

There were worst places to recuperate, and it might not be so bad here for a while.

A bit of quiet for Agatha, and a slow pace for Laura.

Though she longed for the distractions of city life.

She finished her stew and took the remains of her tea outside to see where they were.

Her sisters were nowhere to be seen, but they'd banked a small fire in a shallow pit in the sand, the kettle left nearby.

Claudia was about to top up her tea when she saw a small boy walking along the shore towards her.

Tea forgotten, she watched him walk closer, wondering why he was there, and perhaps what fate he was hoping to dodge.

He approached more quickly than his short legs would suggest, but as he came closer, she realised he was not a boy, but a man.

With sun-bleached hair, and sun-darkened skin.

And muscles of the kind that come from hard work.

Wearing little more than a loincloth.

Walking with the grace and elegance of a panther, perhaps just as dangerous.

He stopped walking a couple of steps away, his arms by his sides and his hands relaxed, looking at her.

Closely.

Curiously.

Confidently.

At the same time as she was looking at him.

Avid. Assessing. Anxious.

She had the sense he could see through her, so she knew he wasn't from this world.

That perhaps the reason he knew, was that finally, she had found another her.

As he completed his examination, he turned and started walking away.

"Wait," she cried.

He stopped but didn't turn back, didn't move at all, just waited.

Nonplussed, she asked the only thing she could think of to stop him leaving, "what is your name?"

He turned his head toward her, and without looking at her said, "there is no need for you to know, as you will not see me again in this lifetime." And started walking again.

"Wait," she said, but he ignored her and kept walking.

He did not acknowledge her presence at all, and she was forced to drop the mug and run after him.

"Wait," she said catching hold of his arm, only to find her grip slid off him as he continued to walk.

"What do you mean in this lifetime?"

He paused for a fraction of a second, so small she barely noticed the check in his stride, and kept walking.

She ran ahead and stopped in his path, three-quarters afraid he'd walk through her body as if it didn't exist and out the other side. And that it would hurt.

But he stopped, considering her once more.

Then he sighed, and said, "you do not belong in this world."

"What makes you say that?"

"I can see your world wrapped around you like a cloak."

She thought about his word choice; wrapped around you like a cloak.

"More like wrapped around my throat like a noose.

"Have you met anyone else like this?"

"No," he said, looking at her with maybe a little more interest.

She put her hands on her hips, "how can you see my world anyway?"

He shrugged, "I don't know. I can just see that you are different to everyone else I have ever met."

"Is everyone else in this world like you?"

"I've never met anyone who is, but that doesn't mean they aren't out there."

She rubbed her eyes and looked at him again.

He didn't have a cloak wrapped around him, but there was something there. Some kind of au-ra.

A kind of buzzing, multicoloured electric aura. That might explain why her hand had slipped off his arm.

"There's something around you too. Some kind of energy that's alive. Something I've never seen before."

"Two of a different kind, but the same. What is this cloak that I see?"

"I am a weaver. My job... Or I suppose my calling is to weave the tapestry of life. My sisters measure and cut the threads."

"Ah, I see. I understand why the cloak is uneven. But why do you say it's like a noose around your neck?"

"Oh," she blushed. "It's all I've ever known, and the way my sisters talk, it's as if the universe would come to an abrupt end if I just let it go."

"I understand. You have no back up. The energy you see in me is the divine energy of this world that connects all creatures. All are one, and one is all, and no one is more important than any other one."

Claudia absently scratched her neck, "I find the idea of all as one oddly comforting. I wonder though, what would happen if I lost my connection to the threads."

"Do you want to find out?"

"Yes."

Without doubt or hesitation.

"Then let me see if I can sever the connection."

He put his hands around her throat, and she felt the burn of his divine energy.

He tightened his grip.

Claudia couldn't breathe and started to feel afraid.

She grappled to get a grip, to loosen his hands, but as with his arms, her hands could find no purchase and just slid off.

She wondered if she could die, and what that would be like. And as she lost consciousness, felt the tiniest bit of regret.

«« • »»

Claudia woke when the tide washed over her legs, with no idea how long the man had been gone, or what he'd done to her, or where she was.

The sun was descending towards a horizon of turquoise water. Tall trees grew down to the pristine white shore, and a light breeze blew down the coast bring the scent of some kind of flowers.

None of which offered any clues about what she was doing in that particular place at that particular time.

She knew there was something important she had to do. When she tried to remember what it was, she couldn't remember who she was Or why the thing she couldn't remember was so important.

She sat up and crawled a little further away from the tide line.

Cold, hungry, clueless.

Trying to work out what was next.

And where she lived.

Circling back to who she was.

Two old ladies were walking up the beach calling out for someone called Claudia, but she paid them no mind until one of them saw her, and started running towards her.

"Claudia, oh thank the gods we found you," the plump black-haired one said. She noticed that the hair on the left side of her head had fallen loose from the woman's bun.

"What the hell happened to you?" demanded the thin white-haired one.

Claudia struggled to close her mouth, then said, "do you know me?"

The women looked at each other, and then the white-haired woman shook her head and offered a hand to help her up. "We do know you, we're your sisters. Why don't you come with us so you can change your wet clothes and get something warm to eat?"

Claudia couldn't help looking at the other woman for confirmation. She nodded and offered her hand as well.

Claudia put up both her hands and allowed the two women to help her up.

The white-haired woman took off a white long-sleeved shirt and went to put it around Claudia's shoulders, and she shrugged it off, saying "don't!"

The old woman choked off a laugh, "at least you haven't forgotten everything."

Weirdly reassured, she followed the women until they disappeared into thin air in front of her.

She gaped, then slowly walked a few steps forward holding her arms out in front of her in case she ran into anything she couldn't see.

Then yelped in surprise as a voice behind her called "Claudia?"

She turned to see the black-haired woman apparently legless, leaning out of nothing.

"She can't see the house," she called to the white-haired woman who put her head out from nowhere to see.

"That's not possible," the white one said, walking further out from the nothing and becoming fully visible.

"Take my hand," she said, and tried to pull Claudia through the nothing to wherever it was the white-haired woman had come from, but the nothing resisted her; wouldn't let her through.

"Something's *really* wrong," she said to the black-haired woman. "We're going to have to get help."

"The night is drawing in; can't we wait until tomorrow?"

"I'm not sure that's wise. We can't take care of her while she's out here. Give me a hand and we'll see if the two of us can get her in here."

The two women, each taking one of her hands were not enough to pull her into the nothing.

"Claudia," said the white-haired woman, "tell me everything you can remember."

"Well, I woke on the beach, but before that...

"Well, I...

"Nope. Can't remember anything from before I woke up just then."

The two women looked at each other again, "Not me bringing you tea?" said the black-haired woman, "or helping you change?" said white.

The black-haired one disappeared and reappeared with some dry red clothes and a mug of something hot, "you know what to do."

They drew aside and watched her change her clothes. She heard something about powers, and stolen, and an old goat.

Though what a cloven-hoofed, ruminant animal had to do with anything she had no idea.

And then they speculated about whether the last trip was too much for her and she'd exhausted her powers.

Something about finding a place and fitting in.

When she'd changed, she looked at them helplessly as she drank her tea.

The white-haired one brought her a bowl of something deliciously savoury, and she let them argue about her some more.

She felt she ought to say something comforting, but there was nothing inside her head to say.

Given their hushed, but urgent tones, they were clearly concerned; trying not to alarm her. Though the whole situation was scaring her more the longer she listened.

What if she never remembered who she was?

What if she never made it back inside her invisible house?

The women seemed kind and concerned about her. Maybe even fond of her.

Now and again, they disagreed and looked at her as if she was the one who always broke the deadlock.

They definitely knew her, and she definitely played an important role in the way they looked at the universe *and* each other.

But she had no idea what.

She looked closely at each of them in turn, but felt no emotional response to either. They could have been anyone.

They *were* anyone. And she wondered whether she could sneak away from them before they noticed, because there was something about them that *really* bothered her.

She yawned, and just for a moment, closed her eyes.

«« • »»

When she woke on the beach the next morning, one or both of them had laid a blanket over her.

They had built a fire and were lying protectively either side of her around the fire.

She snuggled into her blanket, grateful they were near and she had not woken alone.

Her head ached as if someone was very slowly inserting a dagger into her skull. Then suddenly plunged it through, up to the hilt.

She would've screamed, or moved, but she was paralysed by the pain, and couldn't make a sound.

Shortly after that, she passed out.

《《 • 》》

When Claudia woke the second time, she thought perhaps it was a day later.

She bolted upright as she remembered what had happened. Scrambling to her feet and looking around her for the energy man, but he wasn't there.

She turned and looked at her sisters, and saw a tiny hint of multicoloured energy surrounding them, and wondered how they were connected to the divine energy of this world that connected all its creatures.

She looked more closely, and saw they were also connected to each other, and also to her with a red thread of energy, and relaxed. Strangely comforted.

Was he the personification of living energy?

Did that make her the personification of the fate of humanity?

Turning again, she saw the beach shack and understood it was her place. Where she belonged.

She put a pot of water on to boil, and was ready and waiting with tea when they woke.

Agatha examined her, "you're back then?"

Claudia smiled and resisted the temptation to hug her, knowing she'd hate that.

"Really?" asked Laura, and struggling out of her blanket, hugged Claudia, "thank the gods. What happened to you?"

"A stranger showed me my fate."

"Well that sounds positively creepy, should we move somewhere else?" asked Laura.

"Definitely," said Agatha.

"But we came here for you," said Claudia, "somewhere slow-paced and quiet!"

"After yesterday's events, I'd rather not stay here any longer than strictly necessary," Laura declared.

"Agreed," said Agatha, "if you feel up to it."

And oddly, she did, so she nodded.

"Somewhere busy this time," said Agatha.

"Maybe a city where we can go to a show or two," Laura agreed.

Claudia smothered a smile.

They doused the fire and took the blankets and other gear back into the beach shack.

She climbed into her sleeping cupboard as her sisters cleaned up and prepared the shack for travel.

Taking a deep breath, she relaxed into the nexus.

She looked into the tapestry, tracing the thread she'd just emerged from, trying to decide whether to pull it out.

But it unravelled itself and disappeared in a flash of energy.

Which should have annoyed her, but she felt happier that this decision at least had been taken out of her hands.

She picked another thread and followed it, hoping this one would take her back to her sis-ters.

THE END

As a small token of my thanks for reading...

Please enjoy 10% off everything (excluding shipping)

at alexandriablaelock.com

with the code claudiaten.

Turn the page for some ideas where to use it,

Felicia Clarke; influencer.

Old Fashioned. Fiercely independent.

Encourages others, but treads her own path.

Dead, but fondly remembered.

By some.

Get to know Felicaia through these five stories.

The Histories of Hayward Hall

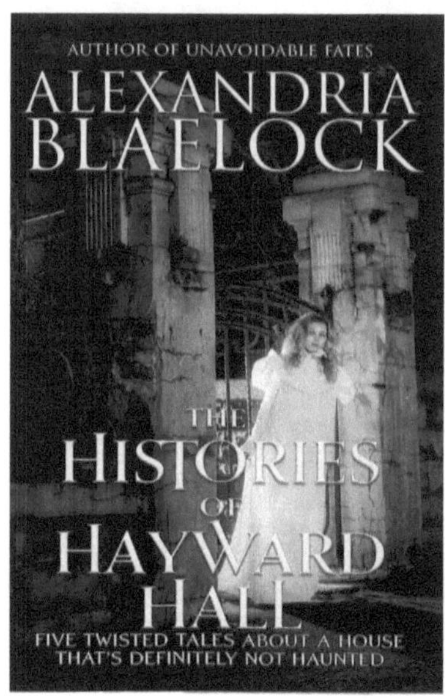

Meet Morag Clementine. The new housekeeper at historic Hayward Hall.

Her practical and capable attitude usually keeps her out of trouble.

bove all, her no-nonsense, get it done approach. And her get in the middle of the scrum outlook. Just as well, because Hayward Hall needs someone like her.

In this genre-spanning collection of original stories, Morag finds herself ensnared in the History of Hayward Hall...

No ordinary housekeeper, can Morag save the house, one century at a time?

Common or Garden Variety Heroes

Do you have what it takes to be a hero?

Whether that's running into a burning building, standing up for what you know is right, or saving the Princess it's going to take everything you've got and more besides.

In this genre-spanning collection of original stories, five women draw on resources they didn't know they had.

Join them, if you dare.

Perhaps you'll carry your new books
in one of these bags

And enjoy them while you're drinking
from one of these mugs

ABOUT THE AUTHOR

Australian author Alexandria Blaelock writes mostly fantasy and mystery.

She's appeared in the Stringybark Anthology *Crowd Surfing*, *Pulphouse Fiction Magazine*, and *Ellery Queen's Mystery Magazine*.

She's also written five self-help books applying business techniques to personal matters like getting dressed, tidying up, and feeding friends.

When not exploring parallel universes, she talks to animals, indulges in K-dramas, and sips Campari. She lives in the Dandenongs, where she relishes the sound of birdsong, the scent of gum leaves and the sun on her face.

Discover more at https://alexandriablaelock.com.

www.ingramcontent.com/pod-product-compliance
Lightning Source LLC
Chambersburg PA
CBHW051829180726
48283CB00004BA/1365